FORGE

NO. 7

 S0-BSO-094

ROUTE 666 CHAPTER 1
Ghouls, ghosts, and girls --
it's Route 666, the horror comic
with the Cold War bite!

MERIDIAN CHAPTER 27
There's a new sheriff in town,
as Sephie takes over Ilahn's estate.

NEGATION CHAPTERS 8 & 9
Lawbringer Qztr whales on
our team of escapees, and
Komptin gets his dog.

THE PATH CHAPTER 6
Obo-san wrestles his demons as
Ryuichi lays siege to the monastery.

SOJOURN CHAPTER 12
Kreeg discovers creepy
monsters in the forest,
while Neven confronts Arwyn.

CRUX CHAPTER 16
Aristophanes and Thraxis
show the CRUX team just how
to take down the Negation!

SURF C.O.W.

www.comicsontheweb.com

Greetings From... WELKIN STATE UNIVERSITY

The Welkin State Campus
COMMONS

KIN STATE
WELKIN STATE GYMNASTICS

STOP
Beautiful Downtown Plainsville

Dear Mr. & Mrs. Starkweather,

WSU Campus Administration wishes to update you on the status of your daughter Cassandra as it pertains to the special purview of this office. Pursuant to information in your daughter's medical history, the Dean of Students requires us to periodically review Cassie's adjustment to her classes and campus living.

Our caseworker is pleased to report that Cassie seems perfectly normal and is doing well academically. Her friend and roommate, Helene Mengert, is deemed a positive influence, as is Cassie's involvement in our nationally recognized gymnastics program.

Naturally, our inquiry was discreet, considering your daughter's very vocal mistrust of standard counseling techniques. You may choose not to reveal that we checked up on her at all. Please rest assured that Cassie's future at WSU looks every bit as bright as our prospects against Towson College at next weekend's gymnastics meet.

Sincerely,
The WSU Office of Mental Health

Tony BEDARD
Writer

Karl MOLINE
Penciler

John DELL
Inker

Nick BELL
Colorist

Troy PETERI
Letterer

WHRR

♪...CHUBBY BURGER TASTES SO FINE...MAKES IT FRESH IN HALF THE TIME...♪

BART! HEY, WHERE YOU GOING?

HOW COME?

SOMETHING I WANTED TO ASK YOU ABOUT-- IN PRIVATE.

?

HURRY UP, CASSIE. I GOTTA WORK ON MY DISMOUNT.

STEP INTO MY OFFICE...

WHRRRRCHNK

HELLO...?

Uh, MISSION CONTROL TO CASSIE...?

YOU GONNA JUST STAND THERE ALL DAY, OR WHAT?

...O-OKAY...

SO, YOU KNOW HOW YOU WERE ASKING ABOUT CASSIE LAST WEEK?

...YEAH?

"WELL, I THINK SHE MIGHT NOT LAUGH IN YOUR FACE IF YOU ASKED HER *OUT.*"

PRETTY *SLOPPY,* MISS STARKWEATHER!

⇒NFF⇐ ...SORRY...

GEE, I DON'T KNOW. MAYBE YOU COULD TELL ME *MORE* ABOUT HER LATER...SAY, OVER *PIZZA* AT GRUMPY'S...?

...

LET ME GUESS: BEER FOR *BREAKFAST?*

Um...I'LL JUST PRETEND YOU DIDN'T *SAY* THAT, BART. CASSIE'S MY FRIEND... MY *BEST* FRIEND... ...AND I REALLY *DO* THINK *YOU TWO* WOULD...YOU KNOW...

LOOK OUT!

UNGH

HEY!

SKZZZ POP

BLEACHER KING

WILL SHE... ...WILL SHE MAKE IT?

WE'LL GET HER THERE AS *FAST* AS WE CAN, MA'AM!

Oh GOD, oh GOD... *I* DID THAT. *I* DID IT...

IT WAS AN *ACCIDENT*, CASSIE. SHE'LL PULL THROUGH.

HOW CAN YOU *KNOW*?! DIDN'T YOU *SEE* HER?!

CASSIE, THE BEST THING YOU CAN DO IS GO HOME.

I'LL FOLLOW THEM TO THE HOSPITAL AND CALL YOU ONCE I *DO* KNOW SOMETHING, OKAY?

VROOM

...O-OKAY... I'LL BE AT MY *PARENTS'* HOUSE.

I CAN'T FACE OUR DORM ROOM RIGHT NOW.

WHAT DO YOU THINK?

SHE'S A GONER. FIVE MINUTES, TOPS.

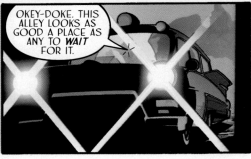

OKEY-DOKE. THIS ALLEY LOOKS AS GOOD A PLACE AS ANY TO *WAIT* FOR IT.

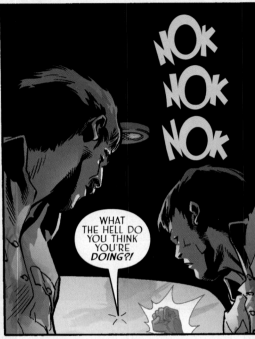

WHY HASN'T SHE *CALLED?*

I'M SURE IT'S BEEN A VERY HARD DAY FOR COACH HOGAN, TOO, SWEETIE.

JUST LEAVE IT TO THE *EXPERTS,* DEAR. HELENE MIGHT STILL BE IN SURGERY.

MAYBE IT'S A *GOOD* SIGN THAT NOBODY'S CALLED YET.

DOCTOR KLASKY PRESCRIBED THESE FOR MY *NERVES.* MAYBE THEY'LL HELP YOU GET SOME *SLEEP,* CASSIE. WE'LL KNOW WHAT'S WHAT BY MORNING.

OKAY, MOM. THANKS.

GET UP! IT WON'T BE LONG...!

NO, NO... I CAN'T...

...I CAN'T DO THIS AGAIN...

SHUT UP AND LISTEN TO ME!

THESE... THESE THINGS ARE AFTER ME AND I DON'T KNOW WHAT TO DO.

I NEED HELP--

Oh, NO...

WHAT...?

SHH. CAN'T YOU HEAR IT?

...YES...

GITCHER SKINNY BUTT BACK HERE RAHT NOW!

HONEY...?

WHAT *HAPPENED?!*

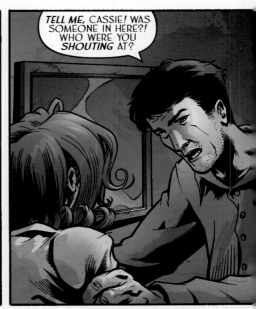

TELL ME, CASSIE! WAS SOMEONE IN HERE?! WHO WERE YOU *SHOUTING* AT?

IT...

...IT WAS *HELENE*. SHE WAS... *DEAD*, BUT...SHE WAS *HERE*, IN MY ROOM!

AND...AND THEN SOME HORRIBLE *THINGS* CAME, AND...AND THEY *TOOK* HER, AND...

Oh.

HONEY, IT'S VERY *NORMAL* TO HAVE A NIGHTMARE AFTER ALL YOU'VE--

NO, DAD!

CALL THE HOSPITAL. SHE'S *DEAD!*

I *KNOW* IT. IT'S...

...IT'S HAPPENING *AGAIN*--JUST LIKE AT TOO-TOO'S *FUNERAL*...

...THE *GOOD* NEWS IS THAT YOU'VE COME TO THE RIGHT PLACE FOR *HELP.*

BUT *I* CAN'T HELP *YOU,* MISS STARKWEATHER, IF YOU AREN'T WILLING TO HELP *YOURSELF.*

...YES, WELL...

...

I UNDERSTAND YOUR RELUCTANCE. AFTER ALL, HOW CAN WE *RATIONALLY* DISCUSS YOUR *EPISODE* LAST NIGHT, WHEN THE WHOLE THING SEEMS SO *IRRATIONAL* TO YOU...YES?

...

WELL...YOU MIGHT BE RELIEVED TO FIND THAT THE THINGS YOU *THINK* YOU SAW OFTEN HAVE A HIDDEN MEANING THAT IS NOT QUITE SO *SINISTER...*

GHOSTS, FOR EXAMPLE, OFTEN SIGNIFY SOME PRESSURE IN YOUR LIFE TO DO SOMETHING YOU DON'T WANT TO. AREN'T YOU GRADUATING FROM COLLEGE NEXT YEAR?

AND, YOU KNOW, A VISION OF A ROAD SIGN IS ALSO INDICATIVE OF AN UPCOMING LIFE CHANGE.

ACCORDING TO YOUR MOTHER, YOU SAW A SIGN THAT READ "ROUTE SIX-SIX-SIX." CAN YOU THINK OF ANY RELEVANCE THAT NUMBER MIGHT HAVE IN YOUR LIFE?

OR PERHAPS IT'S JUST THE REPETITION THAT IS SIGNIFICANT, MM?

MELCHIOR

DOCTOR MELCHIOR'S TIME DOESN'T COME CHEAP, CASSIE. THE MAN'S ASKING YOU A QUESTION, IT'S RUDE NOT TO ANSWER.

OKAY, DAD. SINCE THIS IS ALL ABOUT MONEY, I'LL TALK.

THAT'S NOT WHAT I MEANT.

I KNOW... IT'S JUST...

...IT'S HARD ENOUGH ADMITTING THIS STUFF TO YOU GUYS, MUCH LESS TO HIM.

NO OFFENSE, BUT I DON'T LIKE DOCTORS.

IT'S NOT IMPORTANT IF YOU LIKE ME. I JUST NEED TO KNOW IF I CAN MAKE YOU WELL.

YOUR MOTHER ALSO MENTIONED IMAGINARY PLAYMATES. WHY NOT START THERE?

≈HH≈

YOU ASKED FOR IT...

"...WHEN I WAS AROUND FIVE, I STARTED GETTING *VISITORS* THAT NO ONE ELSE COULD SEE OR HEAR."

"THEY WOULDN'T HAVE FOUND IT SO CUTE, IF I COULD'VE *DESCRIBED* MY INVISIBLE FRIENDS A LITTLE BETTER."

"THEY'D STICK AROUND FOR AN AFTERNOON, OR A COUPLE OF DAYS, THEN *MOVE ON*."

"MOM AND DAD JUST THOUGHT IT WAS A CUTE LITTLE *PHASE* I WAS GOING THROUGH."

"A LOT OF MY FRIENDS HAD SOME PRETTY BIG 'BOO-BOOS,' BUT THEY DIDN'T SEEM TO MIND, SO NEITHER DID I."

"I DIDN'T KNOW WHY THEY CAME TO *ME* IN PARTICULAR, BUT I COULD TELL THAT THEY *FELT* BETTER AROUND ME."

McLANE FUNERAL HOME

"THIS WENT ON FOR A COUPLE OF YEARS. IT *STOPPED* BEING CUTE THE NIGHT OF MY GRANDFATHER'S FUNERAL."

I SEE.

PLEASE FILL OUT THESE *ADMISSIONS FORMS*, MISTER STARKWEATHER. WE SHALL CHECK IN YOUR DAUGHTER *IMMEDIATELY*.

I'LL CALL YOU EVERY NIGHT, AND WE'LL VISIT EVERY WEEKEND! *PROMISE!*

BYE, MOM.

GUSTAV! HELP THE YOUNG LADY TO HER ROOM.

BYE!

RIGHT THIS WAY, SWEET THING. I'LL GIVE YOU THE *NICKEL TOUR.*

NOT UNLESS *CATATONIC* SEEMS OKAY TO YOU.

OH--!

GOD, I THOUGHT YOU WERE THAT SKEEVY *ORDERLY...*

GUS? HE DIDN'T *SAY* OR *DO* ANYTHING... Y'KNOW...?

NO. HE JUST, I DON'T KNOW...SOMETHING ABOUT HIM MAKES MY *SKIN CRAWL.*

WELL, IF *I* COULD GET USED TO HIM, SO CAN YOU.

I'M *DOCTOR WATERMAN.*

SO, UM...AREN'T YOU IN VIOLATION OF MELCHIOR'S STRICT *CREEPS-ONLY* POLICY FOR HIS STAFF?

HA. THAT *"CATATONIC"* CRACK DIDN'T QUALIFY?

JUST KIDDING, SILVIE!

IS SHE REALLY *LISTENING?*

I THINK SHE KNOWS WHEN I'M THERE. AND I THINK SHE LIKES ME. BEYOND THAT? I DOUBT IT.

TRUST ME, SILVIE'S FINE. AS MUCH AS SHE *CAN* BE. I'M MORE CONCERNED WITH *YOU,* MISS STARKWEATHER...

"...I KNOW YOU DON'T WANT TO *BE* HERE, BUT IT'S *MY* JOB TO SHOW YOU THAT THIS ISN'T SUCH A HOUSE OF HORRORS AFTER ALL.

"IT MAY SOUND--PARDON--CRAZY, BUT TRY TO THINK OF YOUR STAY AS A *VACATION.*

"THERE ARE PLENTY OF ACTIVITIES AND THERAPIES TO PUT YOU AT EASE AND BRING YOU OUT OF YOUR *SHELL* A LITTLE.

"JUST KEEP AN OPEN MIND..."

"ONCE I THINK YOU'RE *READY*, WE'LL SCHEDULE SOME PRIVATE SESSIONS WITH DOCTOR M.

"THAT'S WHEN YOU'LL REALLY BE ABLE TO FACE YOUR NEUROSES AND *RESOLVE* THEM."

"SOMEHOW, I *DOUBT* THAT."

"THERE'S SOMETHING *ABOUT* HIM, DOCTOR WATERMAN. SOMETHING THAT JUST FEELS *WRONG*...

"...I MEAN, HAVEN'T YOU EVER MET SOMEONE THAT JUST TURNED YOU OFF RIGHT AWAY?"

"I KNOW, HE'S A PRETTY *COLD FISH*, BUT TAKE MY WORD FOR IT: DOCTOR MELCHIOR RUNS THE *BEST* MENTAL HEALTH PROGRAM IN WELKIN--MAYBE IN ALL EMPYREAN. I'VE BEEN WITH HIM TEN YEARS, AND I'VE SEEN HIM WORK *WONDERS*."

ANYWAY, THIS ISN'T ABOUT *HIM*, IT'S ABOUT *YOU*, MISS STARKWEATHER: *YOU* ARE THE KEY TO THIS WHOLE PROCESS.

YOU'VE MADE PROGRESS IN THESE PAST WEEKS, BUT THE MORE YOU OPEN UP TO US, THE MORE WE CAN *HELP*.

Y'KNOW, YOU CAN CALL ME *CASSIE* IF YOU'D LIKE. "MISS STARKWEATHER" SOUNDS SO *SERIOUS*.

WHAT'S *YOUR* FIRST NAME, DOCTOR WATERMAN?

"DOCTOR."

DON'T EVEN TRY IT. YOU LIKE ME OKAY, I CAN TELL.

→Heh←

YOU *DO* KNOW I'M TRYING TO BE FUNNY, RIGHT...?

CREAK

...uhh...

Uunnnnhh... mmuhhh...

...SILVIE...?

Our Story So Far...

Arwyn

Gareth

Ayden

Neven

The dread warlord Mordath was slain more than three centuries ago, pierced by an arrow shot from the bow of the legendary warrior Ayden. Ayden retreated to the solitude from which he'd come, but broke the fatal arrow into Five Fragments and scattered them to Quin's Five Lands, promising to return should the pieces ever be reunited.

Now Mordath has risen from his tomb. Aided by a sigil that allows him to create and command fire, Mordath has again conquered the Five Lands. One woman, the archer Arwyn, survived her city's destruction at the hands of Mordath's troll armies. Her husband and daughter did not.

Swearing vengeance, Arwyn has taken up the quest to reunite the Five Fragments at the behest of a mysterious and apparently magical woman calling herself Neven. Armed with Ayden's legendary bow and accompanied by the adventurer Gareth and her dog Kreeg, Arwyn has dedicated herself to bringing about Mordath's destruction.

Arwyn began her quest in the land of Middelyn where she discovered the first Fragment in a dragon's treasure hoard. A bargain was struck and the dragon agreed to attack Mordath's castle. But Mordath proved too powerful and slew the beast, while Arwyn and Gareth barely escaped with their lives.

Ron **MARZ** WRITER　June **BRIGMAN** PENCILER　Drew **GERACI** INKER　Jason **LAMBERT** COLORIST　Troy **PETERI** LETTERER

I CAME FOR THE *BOW.*

YOU...

...YOU *WHAT?*

I'M HERE TO *TAKE BACK* AYDEN'S BOW.

YOU TRIED TO CIRCUMVENT THE QUEST. YOU ATTEMPTED TO BRING ABOUT MORDATH'S DESTRUCTION *WITHOUT* GATHERING THE FIVE FRAGMENTS...

...AND YOU *FAILED.* YOU'RE UNFIT TO TAKE UP THIS RESPONSIBILITY.

UNFIT? *YOU'RE* THE ONE WHO CONVINCED ME TO DO THIS. NOW YOU WANT TO—

WAIT. JUST WAIT. GOING AFTER MORDATH WITH THE DRAGON *OBVIOUSLY* DIDN'T TURN OUT THE WAY ANYONE WANTED. BUT WE...

...SHE...

...LEARNED THE LESSON. WE'RE BACK ON THE PATH *YOU* SET US ON.

HRF?

WE'VE *EARNED* THE RIGHT TO CONTINUE, NEVEN.

ESPECIALLY AFTER WHAT WE'VE BEEN THROUGH.

HOW AM I SUPPOSED TO *REMEMBER* WHO YOU ARE?! YOU WON'T *TELL ME!*

YOU'RE JUST SOME *STRANGER* PULLING OUR STRINGS!

YES, I MADE A MISTAKE. AND *YES*, I LEARNED MY LESSON.

BUT I HAVE THE FIRST FRAGMENT. I'M *NOT* STOPPING NOW.

YOU WANT THE BOW...

...YOU *TAKE* IT FROM ME.

GOOD.

GROWF GROWF

KREEG?

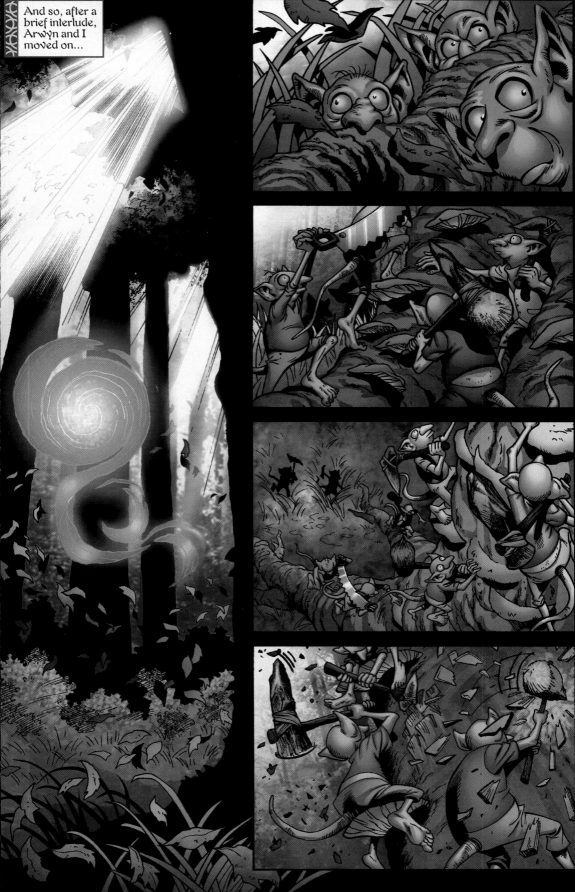

And so, after a brief interlude, Arwyn and I moved on...

...toward the
destinies that
awaited us.

CRUX

CHAPTER 16

THE STORY THUS FAR...

THEY WERE THE ATLANTEANS,

a peaceful civilization of artists and philosophers who used their phenomenal mental and physical skills to build an island utopia. They had but one responsibility: to guide and shepherd Earth's newborn race of *homo sapiens* towards a grand and glorious destiny. But when a mysterious cataclysm plunged Atlantis and its people beneath the waves, six — and only six — were awakened by a nameless stranger one thousand centuries later to find their utopia forgotten and in ruins, their brothers and sisters caught in an unshakeable slumber...and the human race gone, having vanished centuries ago in the Transition, a passage to a higher plane of existence.

The mysterious Atlantean warrior awakened by Tug and Verityn turns out to be Aristophanes, the legendary hero of ancient Atlantis. But introductions are cut short by a new invasion from the Negation universe. At the same time, a more insidious plot from the Negation lures an unwitting Galvan into their clutches.

The mental and physical abilities of the Atlanteans are identical in nature but not in application. Capricia and her teammates have each channeled their abilities into different skills:

CAPRICIA	DANIK	TUG	ZEPHYRE	GALVAN	VERITYN
Shapeshifter and empath	Keeper of the secrets	Telekinetic strongman	Hypermetabolic intellectual	Manipulator of the electromagnetic spectrum	Seer of all truths

Chuck **DIXON** WRITER *Steve* **EPTING** PENCILER *Rick* **MAGYAR** INKER *Frank* **D'ARMATA** COLORIST *Dave* **LANPHEAR** LETTERER

...HE'S NOT AN ENEMY OF ATLANTIS. HE NEVER *WAS*.

THRAXIS WAS A *SLAVE* TO THE UGLIES WHO RAN THIS SHIP.

THAT'S HIS *NAME*--

THRAXIS?

"--I THINK."

GET *BACK*, ZEPH!

YOU'LL BE PULLED IN, TOO!

I-- *CAN'T!*

YOU *HAVE* TO!

--UNNH!--

STAY *AWAY*, ZEPH! STAY *AWAY!*

GALVAN--

--I *LOVE* YOU!

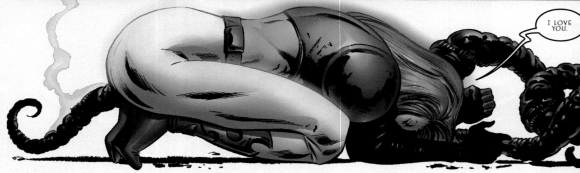

I *LOVE* YOU.

"--DOESN'T *ANYONE* STAND STILL ANYMORE?"

NO!

YOU'VE *RELEASED* THE BEAST! YOU'VE DOOMED US *ALL!*

GET 'EM, THRAXIS! *YOU* CAN DO IT!

THAT MONSTER IS TEN *TIMES* THE SIZE OF YOUR NEW FURRY FRIEND.

THRAXIS CAN WHIP THAT UGLY! HE'S GOT *HEART!*

DO I REALLY HAVE TO *REMIND* YOU--

--THAT CREATURE IS *NOT* A PET.

NEVER ALLOW AN ENEMY TO RETIRE FROM THE FIELD.

WE MUST HARRY THEM TO THE *LAST!*

THAT MAN IS *INSANE.*

WITHOUT HIM AND THRAXIS YOU MIGHT BE DEAD.

THRAXIS?

THEY'RE *ROUTED!* THEIR SPIRIT *BROKEN!*

WE MUST *CARRY* THE BATTLE TO THEM!

THEY MUST BE EXTERMINATED!

HE'S
GONE.

WELL, THAT CONFIRMS
THAT THE LEGENDS ABOUT
HIM ARE TRUE.

I ALMOST
FEEL SORRY
FOR THE ENTIRE
NEGATION
UNIVERSE.

TOO MUCH.
IT'S ALL
MOVING TOO
SWIFTLY.

FOR ALL OF
US. WHAT'S
THIS ABOUT
DANIK?

I'LL
MAKE YOU A
DEAL, TUG.

LET ME REST FOR
A MOMENT AND I'LL
EXPLAIN AS MUCH
AS I CAN.

AND
YOU'LL TELL
ME WHERE WE ARE
AND WHAT THAT
THING IS...

"...BUT FOR RIGHT NOW I'M JUST *EXHAUSTED*."

WELL...

...HOPE THERE'S SOME *FOOD* HERE.

EVEN SOME TERRA COGNITO SEMI-BURGERS WOULD GO DOWN GOOD ABOUT--

♪ ♪ ♪

Uh?

MERIDIAN ™

Brigman·Geraci·MO!

CHAPTER 27

Far away, on the world of Demetria, explosions rocked the surface and gigantic rocks shot into the sky and stayed there. Settlers established great city-states on these ore-buoyant islands, using floating ships to move between them.

One of these islands is Meridian, home of shipbuilders and Sephie, the daughter of Minister Turos. Sephie has become the Minister of Meridian after her father's death. Her uncle Ilahn is the Minister of the rich city-state of Cadador, which controls most of the shipping and trade on Demetria.

A mysterious force has endowed both Sephie and Ilahn with power — opposing forces — Ilahn's destruction versus Sephie's renewal.

Ilahn wants to control Sephie — and Meridian — but Sephie has been fighting to resist Ilahn's control of herself and Demetria's commerce. The conflict between them erupts into a battle, during which Ilahn disappears...apparently dead at Sephie's hands. Sephie returns to Meridian only to find herself leaving the island again to go to Cadador, which she intends to rule.

Barbara
KESEL
WRITER

June
BRIGMAN
Guest PENCILER

Tom
SIMMONS
INKER

Morry
HOLLOWELL
COLORIST

Troy
PETERI
LETTERER

Seeing Cadador again made me shudder.

I didn't want to return to that island, ever, but I'd been provided an opportunity that couldn't be wasted.

So I returned to Cadador...

...this time, to rule it.

ISN'T CADADOR'S PORT BELOW THE RIM OF THE ISLAND?

WE'RE NOT ANCHORING IN THE DOCKS -- WE'LL TIE OFF ON THE RAIL AROUND ILAHN'S ESTATE.

THIS ENTIRE ISLAND IS...WAS HIS HOME.

BUT MORE PEOPLE WILL *SEE* YOUR ARRIVAL IF YOU PUT INTO PORT, SEPHIE.

YOU REALLY OUGHT TO LET THEM SPREAD THE STORY FOR YOU.

MORE PEOPLE WILL HEAR ABOUT IT IF I TAKE THE ESTATE.

THE GOSSIP CHAIN FROM ILAHN'S ESTATE IS THE MOST EFFICIENT COMMUNICATION SYSTEM ON CADADOR.

Nervous as I was, I knew I was ready for this.

Papa had made sure I'd be ready.

Did he ever suspect? About Ilahn?

I DO ALWAYS APPRECIATE YOUR ADVICE, DEREN, BUT THIS ISN'T ABOUT SPREADING A RUMOR.

THIS IS ABOUT ASSERTING POLITICAL POWER.

CROWD CONTROL IS *YOUR* SPECIALTY--

STATECRAFT IS *MINE*.

They say there are two steps to training an eguassa. First, you've got to get its attention.

Not that the people of Cadador are likely to start pulling carts and carriages...

...but the principle is the same.

CUT THOSE LINES! YOU CAN'T MOOR HERE!

Those who had met me here knew me only as Ilahn's cowed niece.

They had to learn to see ME as Minister.

So I had to get their attention.

...NISTER OF
ADADOR.

OH, NO, LOROSI--
YOU'RE STAYING
WITH US.

WE'LL LET SEPHIE
EXPLORE A LITTLE
ON HER OWN...

"...LET HER GET TO KNOW
THE PLACE AGAIN."

...back when I
was happy.

"adador holds so
many memories...

...from long ago,
before I was
Minister...

...before
the sigil...

SEPHIE?

OH!

I-- I WAS
JUST...

...REMEMBERING.

GOOD
MEMORIES, FROM
THE LOOKS OF IT.

MOSTLY...

Cadador holds memories, but it also holds so many secrets. Its reputation for deceit and underhanded dealings extends back centuries.

IT *IS!* IT'S MY MOTHER'S ARTWORK!

WHAT A COLLECTION! DID YOU SPEND MUCH TIME HERE, SEPHIE?

NO... I WASN'T ALLOWED BACK HERE. THIS IS ILAHN'S PRIVATE WING.

ILAHN'S? ITS DESIGN DOESN'T MATCH THE REST OF THE HOUSE.

ILAHN WAS BRIEFLY MARRIED. THIS LIBRARY MAY HAVE BEEN CLAIRESSA'S.

WHAT'S THIS? CRENNER, IT LOOKS LIKE--!

ILAHN, CADADOR'S FORMER MINISTER, APPEARS TO BE DEAD. IN HIS ABSENCE, CADADOR BECOMES MINE TO RULE BY RIGHT OF SUCCESSION.

APPEARS TO BE DEAD?

BUT WITNESSES HEARD YOU SAY *YOU* KILLED HIM!

ILAHN HAD GONE MAD.

HE THREATENED MERIDIAN WITH THE SAME FATE AS TORBEL.

WOULD THE LOSS OF *ANOTHER* ISLAND HAVE BEEN GOOD FOR CADADOR'S BUSINESS?

NEVERTHELESS, CADADOR CANNOT ALLOW ASSUMPTION OF HER MINISTRY TO BE ACHIEVED THROUGH MURDER.

OOOH!

YOU KILLED YOUR UNCLE TO LAY CLAIM TO CADADOR!

DO YOU THINK WE'LL STAND IDLY BY WHILE YOU PROFIT FROM YOUR CRIME?

COUNCILOR...

KRNNCH   KRNNCH

AIEEEEE!

AYAAAH!

EEEE!

ARE YOU ALL PREPARED TO *LISTEN* NOW?

GOOD.

ALLOW ME TO OUTLINE A FEW SIMPLE CHANGES I'LL BE MAKING TO CADADOR'S DAILY OPERATIONS.

NOTHING SUBSTANTIAL WILL BE ALTERED, BUT THE PROPORTIONS OF PROFIT ARE INEQUITABLY BIASED TOWARD CADADOR AT THE EXPENSE OF TOO MANY NEIGHBOR CITIES.

CURRENT AGREEMENTS ARE STRUCTURED FOR EXCELLENT SHORT-TERM RETURN, BUT ARE DAMAGING TO LONG-TERM RELATIONSHIPS WITH CITIES WE WILL NEED ON OUR SIDE IN ORDER TO SUSTAIN CADADOR'S SUPPLY CHAIN AS THE TOXIC REGIONS EXPAND.

THIS ISLAND PRODUCES NONE OF ITS OWN FOOD OR FUEL, REMEMBER.

WE NEED TO ACT QUICKLY TO REPAIR AND STRENGTHEN RELATIONSHIPS NOW THAT WILL BE CRUCIAL TO OUR FUTURE.

DON'T WORRY. YOU'LL ALL STAY RICH... BUT A LITTLE LESS SO.

THOSE PEOPLE ARE ALL SQUIRMING LIKE THEIR CLOTHES ARE TOO TIGHT.

IT'S THE FIRST TIME THEY'VE EVER BEEN TALKED TO LIKE *THAT*, I'M SURE.

I'M NOT SURE IT'S A GOOD IDEA FOR SEPHIE TO BE SO FORCEFUL WITH THEM--

SHE NEEDS TO WIN THEIR TRUST.

THIS IS *CADADOR*, NOT PEACEFUL ANHEIM.

LIKE TO LIKE -- SHE SEES WHAT CONNECTS.

YES, SHE'S FOUND THE SHORTCUT TO... DOMINATING THE NEGOTIATION, BUT IF THEY LEARN TO HATE HER, THEY'LL NEVER VOLUNTARILY ASSIST HER.

SHE WILL FIND HERSELF FACING MUCH MORE THAN AN ANGRY COUNCIL...SHE MUST BE *READY*.

READY FOR WHAT? MUSE, WHAT DO YOU *SEE* FOR HER?

IS THERE ANYTHING *I* CAN DO TO HELP HER?

HMMM...

WHAT *DO* I SEE FOR YOU?

THERE! THAT'S DONE!

NOW I'M OFF TO CONVINCE WHAT'S LEFT OF CADADOR'S SOLDIERS THAT I REALLY HAVE TAKEN CHARGE.

AREN'T YOU GONNA LET US HELP?

WHEN YOU CAN *FLY*, COTSON!

SERIOUSLY, THIS HAS TO BE JUST ME -- IF I SHOW UP IN THE PRESENCE OF ADULTS, IT WON'T MATTER WHAT I SAY *OR* DO --

-- THEY WON'T LISTEN TO THE *GIRL*.

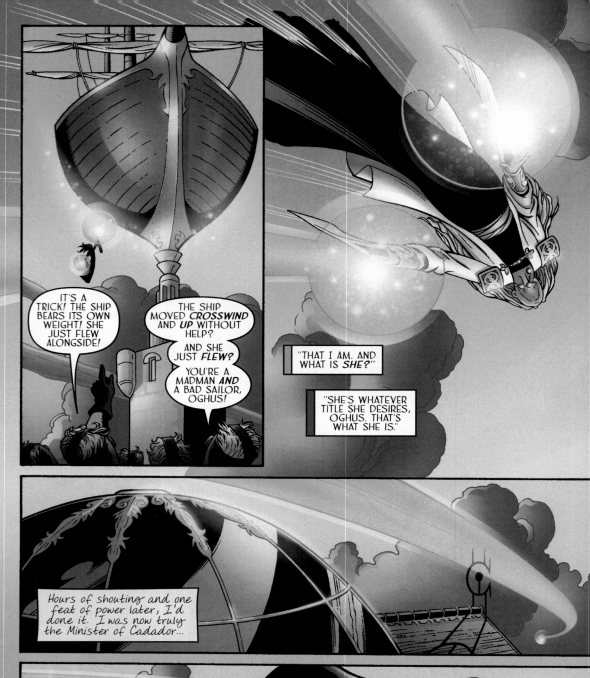

IT'S A TRICK! THE SHIP BEARS ITS OWN WEIGHT! SHE JUST FLEW ALONGSIDE!

THE SHIP MOVED *CROSSWIND* AND *UP* WITHOUT HELP?

AND SHE JUST *FLEW?*

YOU'RE A MADMAN *AND* A BAD SAILOR, OGHUS!

"THAT I AM. AND WHAT IS *SHE?*"

"SHE'S WHATEVER TITLE SHE DESIRES, OGHUS. THAT'S WHAT SHE IS."

Hours of shouting and one feat of power later, I'd done it. I was now truly the Minister of Cadador...

...and, in llahn's absence, there was no one who could challenge me for the role.

THE PATH

CHAPTER 6

THUS FAR

ON THE PATH...

The monk Obo-san refused to surrender the Weapon of Heaven to Emperor Mitsumune, ruler of Nayado. In a fit of madness, or perhaps sanity, Mitsumune committed ritual suicide and was resurrected, commanding Obo-san's death. Obo-san and his companions, Wulf and Aiko, escaped to a northern monastery, to which General Ryuichi laid siege. As Wulf and Obo-san plotted strategy, demons melted from the monastery shadows.

Ron **MARZ**
WRITER

Bart **SEARS**
PENCILER

Mark **PENNINGTON**
INKER

Michael **ATIYEH**
COLORIST

Dave **LANPHEAR**
LETTERER

WE DON'T EXPECT MUCH RESISTANCE FROM THE VILLAGE. IT'S MOSTLY WOMEN AND OLD MEN.

WE'RE ROUNDING THEM UP TO MAKE CERTAIN NO ONE ESCAPES AND SPREADS NEWS OF THE INVASION.

GOOD...

THIS MISERABLE SCRAP OF AN ISLAND WILL BELONG TO THE AUGUST EMPIRE WITHIN THE WEEK.

I WANT THIS WRAPPED UP AS QUICKLY AS POSSIBLE.

UNDERSTOOD?

YES, SIR.

WE MARCH ON YAZAKI IMMEDIATELY...

"...AND WHEN WE GET THERE I'LL HAVE MITSUMUNE'S HEAD AS MY TROPHY."

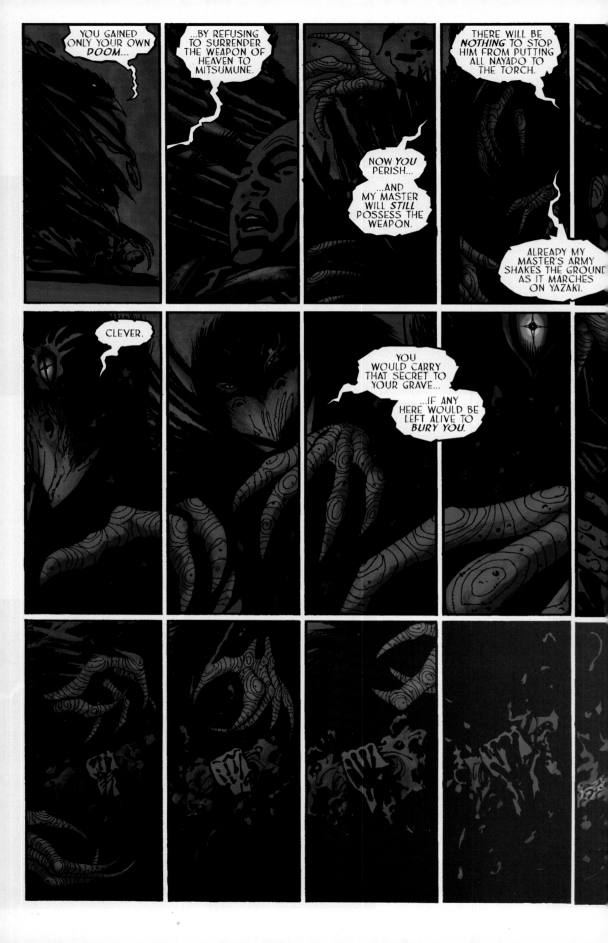

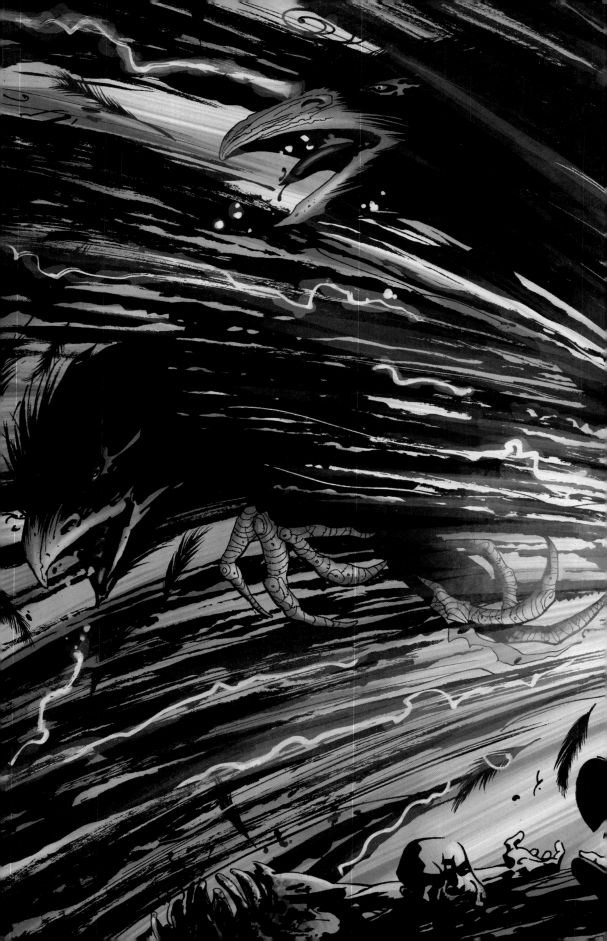

OBO-SAN, ARE YOU *HURT*?

I USED IT...

WHAT?

I *USED* IT. I USED THE WEAPON.

WHAT... HAPPENED?

IT *DESTROYED* THEM.

THAT ONE REELS FROM ITS WOUNDS...

...BUT IT *LIVES*.

AND IT THINKS TO *ESCAPE!*

Hmf.

Hn?

OBO-SAN?

OBO-SAN, COME **HERE!** RYUICHI'S ARMY...

SHINACEA'S HORDES HAVE AGAIN BREACHED OUR SHORES.

RYUICHI MUST HAVE RECEIVED WORD AND GOES TO MEET THEM, THOUGH HE WILL BE SORELY OUTNUMBERED.

OBO-SAN, **HOW?** HOW COULD YOU POSSIBLY KNOW THIS?

THE DEMON...

...YUKIO...

...REVEALED IT TO ME. SHINACEA MARCHES UPON YAZAKI.

Negation

CHAPTER 8

KAINE

The God-Emperor CHARON conquered His chaotic universe and forged an intergalactic empire known as:

the NegaTion

Charon now casts His baleful eye across the gulf between realities and covets the bright and thriving worlds in *our* cosmos.

On His orders, one hundred strangers were abducted from our universe and brought to His dark realm to be studied and tested on a harsh prison-world. Some captives, such as the pirate Mercer Drake and the constable Shassa, bore a mysterious mark of power known as the Sigil, granting them astonishing abilities. Others, such as the godlike Evinlea, were inherently powerful. Most, however, were simple, ordinary humans.

One such human named Obregon Kaine led a bloody uprising against the Negation prison warden, Komptin. The few captives who escaped along with Kaine wander the hostile stars, seeking a way home.

Now Charon's most feared enforcer, Lawbringer Qztr, confronts the escapees in an abandoned alien settlement. Nothing the fugitives have ever seen can prepare them for this terrifying foe...

DRAKE

EVINLEA

CHARON

KOMPTIN

QZTR   SHASSA

TONY **BEDARD** WRITER   PAUL **PELLETIER** PENCILER   DAVE **MEIKIS** INKER   JAMES **ROCHELLE** COLORIST   TROY **PETERI** LETTERER

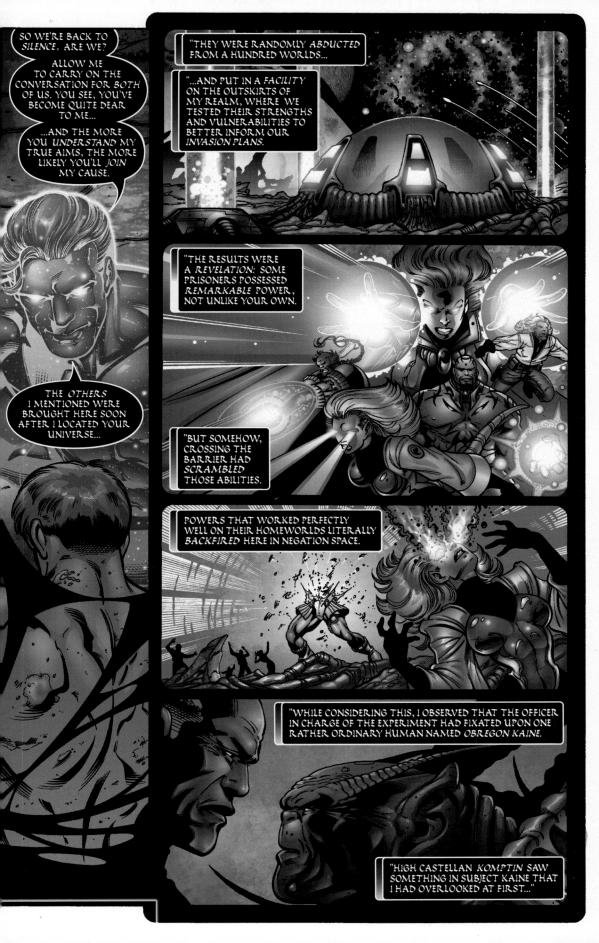

"SUCH SPIRIT, CUNNING AND LEADERSHIP IN ONE SO...*ORDINARY* PROVED QUITE FASCINATING.

"WHEN KOMPTIN RASHLY TRIED TO DESTROY THIS MOST INTRIGUING SPECIMEN, I INTERCEDED.

"MY *MANIFESTATION* IS ENOUGH TO FRIGHTEN SOME FOR A *LIFETIME*, BUT NOT KAINE. SOON AFTER, HE ORCHESTRATED A MASS *ESCAPE*.

"I *ALLOWED* IT TO HAPPEN. LETTING THEM *SUCCEED* WAS PROVING FAR MORE INSTRUCTIONAL THAN KEEPING THEM *CAGED*.

"KAINE'S BAND OF ESCAPEES SOON JOINED THE FUGITIVE CREW OF A LOCAL VESSEL.

"AS FOR KOMPTIN, HE'S BEEN TRYING TO RECAPTURE THEM EVER SINCE.

"HIS BLIND HATRED OF KAINE HAS DRIVEN HIM TO SURPRISING EXTREMES.

"FOR EXAMPLE, HE ENTICED ONE OF MY *LAWBRINGERS*, TO AID HIM, OFFERING HIM THE DEMIGODDESS *EVINLEA* AS HIS PRIZE."

BUT EVEN MY FAITHFUL LAWBRINGER QZTR IS MISSING THE *POINT* IF HE THINKS EVINLEA IS THE MOST DANGEROUS OF OUR RUNAWAYS.

IT'S *KAINE* HE SHOULD KEEP AN EYE ON...

THE ONE NAMED *EVINLEA* WILL STEP FORWARD AND DEPART WITH ME.

THE REST OF YOU WILL *REMAIN* HERE AND... ...AND...

WHAT?

WHAT *IS* IT?

Oh.

BUT *WHAT?*

WELL, SIR, WE'RE ALL WONDERING WHY WE'RE *HERE.* LAWBRINGER QZTR ORDERED US TO MAINTAIN A PATROL TWO SECTORS AWAY.

SIR, WE'VE ESTABLISHED CONTACT WITH THE CIVIL COMM-SYSTEM ON KALIMA, BUT...

AS SOON AS QZTR GETS TIRED OF PLAYING WITH THE FUGITIVES, HE'LL CALL US IN TO COLLECT WHOEVER'S LEFT ALIVE. WHEN HE DOES, IF PRISONER KAINE IS STILL BREATHING...WELL...

LET'S JUST SAY I'LL HAVE A *SURPRISE* WAITING FOR HIM.

NOW I NEED TO MAKE A *PRIVATE* CALL. DO NOT, FOR *ANY* REASON, INTERRUPT ME. UNDERSTOOD?

⇒HH⇐

Oh, FOR CHARON'S SAKE...

PEEP PEEP PEEP

CALL BACK -- I'M *BUSY!*

THAT'S A HELL OF A WAY TO ANSWER THE PHONE, *KAMFIR.*

PUT *MOTHER* ON.

KOMPTIN? IS THAT YOU?! WHAT ARE *YOU* CALLING FOR?

I *TOLD* YOU I WANT TO SPEAK WITH MOTHER.

FORGET IT. I AM *THIS* CLOSE TO BEATING MY TOP SCORE. I'M NOT MOVING FOR ANYTHING.

HAVE SOME RESPECT AND *LOOK* AT ME WHEN YOU SPEAK!

GO GET RESPECT FROM THE NEGATION! *THEY'RE* YOUR FAMILY NOW!

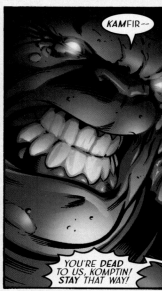

KAMFIR--

YOU'RE *DEAD* TO US, KOMPTIN! *STAY* THAT WAY!

WHOA! DID YOU *SEE* THAT?! *TRIPLE BONUS!*

ALL RIGHT, LITTLE BROTHER. YOU'VE GROWN UP ENOUGH NOW TO TAKE *RESPONSIBILITY* FOR YOUR DECISIONS.

SO UNDERSTAND *THIS:* IF YOU DON'T PUT MOTHER ON THE PHONE *RIGHT NOW...*

...I SWEAR BY HOLY CHARON THAT I WILL COME DOWN THERE IN PERSON...

...AND *FEED* YOU YOUR OWN *EYEBALLS.*

SO, KAMFIR **WAS** TELLING THE TRUTH...

HELLO, MOTHER.

"HELLO"--? IS THAT **ALL** YOU HAVE TO SAY FOR YOURSELF?

MOM...!

I **KNOW** YOU'RE PROBABLY WONDERING WHY I NEVER GOT IN TOUCH AFTER I **ENLISTED.**

EIGHT YEARS WITHOUT A WORD FROM ME, NOT EVEN WHEN **FATHER** DIED.

I'M **SURE** YOU FEEL YOU DESERVE AN **EXPLANATION...**

...BUT I REALLY **COULDN'T** CARE LESS.

THEN WHAT DO YOU **WANT** FROM ME?

I'M HERE TO PICK UP **GULLIT.**

GULLIT.

ARE YOU **SURE...**?

POSITIVE. MEET ME AT THE VAULT IN AN HOUR.

OKAY, YOU'RE HEALED. READY TO TAKE ON THAT MONSTER?

DON'T LET GO, JAVI. PRETEND YOU'RE *STILL* HEALING ME.

BUT...

LOOK...I DON'T KNOW IF WE CAN *BEAT* HIM--! I'M...

JAVI, I'M *AFRAID.*

SCUTTLING...

...SCURRYING...

...VERMIN...

ALL OF YOU-- *STOP!*

>WHULP<

YOU DISGUST ME.

>UHH<

YOUR... SCURRYING... INSULTS THE DIGNITY OF THIS MOMENT.

MANY OF YOU AREN'T EVEN WORTH BOTHERING WITH.

N-NO! LET GO OF ME!

WHO ARE YOU TO JUDGE US? B-BY WHAT RIGHT DO YOU--

I WAS BIRTHED TO PUNISH THE FAITHLESS AND TEST THE MIGHTY.

IF YOU ARE MUNDANE, THEN YOU ARE JUST CLUTTER...

Y-YOU CAN BLEED ME EASY ENOUGH, Y'UGLY BLUDGER... BUT YOU SHAN'T ESCAPE YOUR OWN PUNISHMENT!

DRAKE AND M-MISTRESS SHASSA WILL HAVE AT YOU RELENTLESSLY-- --HAMMER AND TONG, TOOTH AND N-NAIL...!

HAMMER?

NAIL?

Ah.

THRUNCH

>NFF<...SHASSA... SOMEBODY... PLEASE...

URRRR...

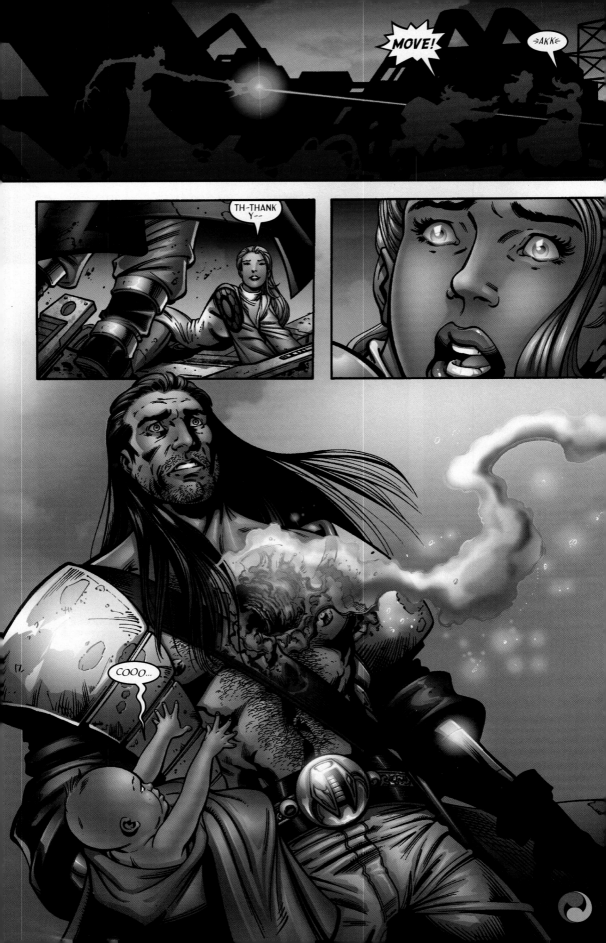

Ah.

OUR ONLY HOPE IS TO HIT HIM ALL *TOGETHER!*

C'MON, EVINLEA!

BUT--

NOTHING *FANCY*--

WESTIN! GET TO THE *SHIP* AND START HER UP! TIME TO *SKY* OUTTA HERE!

WON'T THAT THING JUST *CRUNCH* US LIKE A CHUG-CAN ONCE WE'RE ALL INSIDE?

NOT IF HE'S *DISTRACTED.* ME AND EVINLEA CAN TAKE CARE OF *THAT!*

EVERYBODY GET TO THE *SHIP!* WE'RE DUSTING OFF *ASAP!*

GET HER OUT OF HARM'S WAY, MATUA! I'LL--

STIMULATING. MY MOST STIMULATING ENCOUNTER IN A VERY, *VERY* LONG TIME.

GET YOUR FILTHY HANDS *OFF ME!*

LOOK OUT!

WRONG WAY, KAINE!

WHERE'S ZAIDA?

LORDS OF HALGEDAE... WHY TAKE *JAVI*... WHY *HIM*?

ZAIDA! HIT THE--

SHRANT

--DECK--!

...ZAIDA...

...MEMI...

MURDERER! COWARD! BABY KILLER!

SO...YOU'VE ACTUALLY COME TO *CARE* FOR THESE *VERMIN*...?

GET EVERYONE INTO THE SHIP AND *GO*. EVINLEA AND I WILL STAY BEHIND AND KEEP THE LAWBRINGER BUSY.

DOES... *SHE* KNOW YOU'RE VOLUNTEERING HER TO DIE...?

THAT THING'S *OBSESSED* WITH HER -- SHE'S DEAD ALREADY.

AAHHH -- WAHHHHH....!

Eh?

FINAL CHANCE TO *RECONSIDER.*

HROONK

I CAN *HANDLE* HIM, MOTHER. I'VE *CHANGED.*

→SIGH←

NOT REALLY. I *STILL* CAN'T TELL YOU A THING.

I JUST HOPE YOU *WARNED* YOUR MEN.

YEAH, YEAH...

WHRRR

K-CHNK

ZZZK

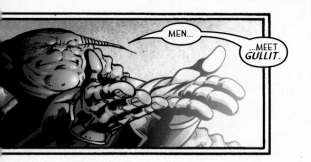

GYAOWWWRRL!

HREENK*

HREEK*

SHREDDER--!

FALL BACK! FALL BACK!

GOOD DOG, GULLIT. YOU REMEMBER ME, RIGHT? YES... YES YOU DO...

WELL... AT LEAST IT WON'T BE ON OUR PLANET ANYMORE...

ARRR!

≤WHUNG≥

THE SENTENCE FOR HERESY IS--

NO, QZTR. THIS ONE STILL SERVES OUR PURPOSES.

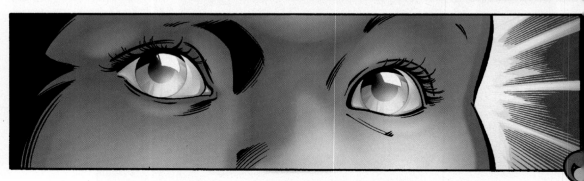

Bart Sears has been a professional comics artist since 1985. Since then he's worked for just about every major company penciling just about every marquee character. Bart started teaching at the Joe Kubert School in 1990 and wrote a 'How To' column for *Wizard* magazine for three years. He also drew a lot of the early Wizard covers and helped establish that magazine's look.

In the late 1990s Bart went to work for Hasbro as a toy designer, but he kept a hand in comics on titles like Marvel's *Blade* and *Spider-Woman*. Bart arrived at CrossGen in time to launch THE FIRST before moving on to start THE PATH. Bart has since become CrossGen's Art Director.

Whereas his work on THE FIRST is bright and bursting with energy, THE PATH is dark, almost gloomy, and rarely do the figures seem fully defined. Yet for all that THE PATH has a vibrant, kinetic quality that stands out from the rest of Bart's work.

How would you characterize your approach to THE PATH? It looks so different from your past work.

Yeah, it is a big departure. Instead of focusing on ultra-realistic muscular figures, I'm creating tension and motion with black shapes.

I've been drawing hyper-muscular stuff for most of my life, but that's never been something I completely enjoyed. Superheroes are fine – the heroic part at least – but when the muscles are the focus, the storytelling suffers. Whereas in THE PATH, visual storytelling is the most important thing.

It's a matter of getting closer to the comics I personally enjoy. I've always liked Frank Miller's work, especially the *Sin City* stuff. What first attracted me to it is that Miller stopped trying to draw pretty. He concentrated instead on the storytelling, which was purer because it wasn't glossed up. At this phase of his career he's getting to the essence of graphic storytelling. Every element Miller puts on the page helps tell his story. There's nothing extra. Nothing wasted.

He seems to groove on taking things down to their bare essentials.

And yet at the same time there's plenty of eye candy in Miller's black and white work. The way he uses rain, for instance. He's constantly warping light and space to create a dramatic effect that's not entirely realistic. It's not the same as super-realistic muscles, but it's eye candy that establishes mood and therefore fits the story.

I'm taking a similar approach in THE PATH. I'm not using light realistically. I'm using black primarily to enhance the design of the page and set the mood of the story. Even in my layouts, I'm less interested in displaying an activity than in building drama. A lot of stuff happens off panel. I'll do panels where the only thing you see of the main character is his cheek. All to enhance the dramatic tension.

Miller was one of the first American artists to study Japanese cartooning and try to incorporate some of their approaches in his own work. Are you a manga fan?

Not really. I do read *Lone Wolf & Cub*, which I've always enjoyed. It contains some of the best references for everyday things within that time period. But *Lone Wolf & Cub* is just about the only manga I've read.

Alex Toth has really influenced my approach to THE PATH. Toth is another master of blacks. He's a guy who doesn't go for the eye candy. His simplicity of line and layouts are just beautiful. And he's a fantastic visual storyteller.

To my mind, when you're reading a comic, if you ever have to stop reading the story to stare at the beautiful rendering an artist has put there, then the artist has failed. He's pulled you out of the story. We've all done it countless times. That's the fine line we cross daily when we make comics. And that's one thing I'm trying to get away from in THE PATH.

Are you saying an artist shouldn't put beauty on the page? That there's no room for detail in comics?

I'm saying that the best graphic stories you read without necessarily noticing the art – and that's when the art is most successful.

If you're watching TV and somebody's talking to you, that distraction to me is the same type of distraction as when you've stopped reading to look at the beautiful art. If the art is so exquisitely rendered that it takes you out of the story being told, then the artist has failed.

We've all sat in the movie theater watching a film so bad we started noticing the special effects. But some movies do the opposite. The story is so good and the storytelling so seamless that you only notice the great special effects in hindsight. That's what I'm aiming for in THE PATH.

How do you achieve this spareness, when your work has always been known for hyper-realistic detail?

The essence of my art has always been structure – the basic form over which you construct the figure. Generally, you start with a basic form and keep adding layers of muscle, rendering, costume detail, all that stuff. With every layer of detail, you run the risk of overwhelming the basic form, removing its essential weight and motion.

What I'm doing with THE PATH is putting down a basic form, then choosing the simplest, quickest, thickest black shapes I can put on that form to define the figure. With your first look, you get it immediately. You shouldn't have to figure out the details of a guy's costume to know who he is or what he's doing. And there should be some weight behind the figure. His structure should be sound.

The tool I use most when I'm penciling this book is a thick black marker. Come to think of it, I don't really use a pencil on THE PATH at this point. I do a small half-size page layout, and then I just start with the markers. I do everything with the markers and black shapes, which keeps me concentrated on structure.

If you're drawing in ink, how does your inker earn his pay?

Right now we're scanning my half-size pages, which are very rough – I mean they're not meant to be finished pages. We scan them in, enlarge them 200%, print them out as bluelines, and Mark [Pennington] inks that.

Mark is truly inking on THE PATH. In fact, you could call him a 'finisher.' Mark needs to interpret every single line. There's no tracing at all on that board.

Penciling has become such an anal-retentive medium, where pencilers put down every single line to be inked. Then the inker is supposed to trace those pages. I think that's bull. At least, that's the opposite of how I want to work here.

Earlier you mentioned that your spare approach made it easier to capture motion in your figures. Can you expand on that?

The sparer your penciling is, the less rendered, the easier it is to convey action. A simple line and heavy blacks enhance the motion you can convey in a drawing. I think it falls back to the speed with which your eye sees the image.

I've always felt constrained by a pencil. It comes to a point, and it's made for drawing fine lines. I've drawn a few books in the past where I've used blunt pencils, with soft lead, to try to get more energy and power in a simpler line. I've found with THE PATH that the fat markers are even better for that. If I had to render it in pencil, I'm sure I would noodle it up and add a lot of extraneous rendering and detail. But with the markers there are no do-overs, and that cuts out extraneous detail.

Plus, when I'm penciling with markers and I screw up, I just draw a new panel and paste that over. I try to put the blacks in as quick as I can, because, if I don't, I may overthink it, and that'll make the panel stiff.

For the first four or five issues of THE PATH, I actually enlarged my half-page marker breakdowns, then traced over them with pencil, and that's what I sent to Mark. But Mark convinced me that I was losing a lot of the energy and life of the marker drawings, so we tried blowing up the marker drawings for him to ink, and that's worked just fine.

With THE PATH, you've definitely chosen the double-page spread as your main storytelling unit and the horizontal panel as your design conceit. Why?

Part of it was to keep my interest level up. I've been doing this a long time, and I'm bored with single-page layouts. So the two-page spread is a huge

challenge. In THE PATH, it allows for a kind of widescreen storytelling. I can do long thin horizontal panels that have tremendous scope and huge vistas. It also lets me break some hard and fast storytelling rules, which is fun. For instance, in the middle of the page, I may have a series of panels that you can read top to bottom, but don't break up your natural left-to-right reading flow.

Remember that episode of *Seinfeld*, where George kind of goes against everything he usually does? He just does the opposite. And that makes him successful – he gets the women, and the job, and everything. That's sort of how I approach THE PATH.

For instance, on this spread my first instinct was to have the largest panel or the major focus of the spread be the fight. Instead, I chose to make the largest panel the aftermath of the fight, when Todosi sheathes his sword. And the fight I broke up and conveyed with smaller, thinner panels, which create more chaos and energy. You want to see more, but you can't, and that gives the sequence a kind of nervous charge. It makes you antsy, because you can't really tell what's happening. I like to think it makes for a truer depiction of battle.

And what is happening in this middle tier of panels?

It's quick cuts. In a two-page spread, you can have a large panel on the left side and a large panel on the right, and then between them you can have several horizontal panels in the same tier without confusing the reading flow of a page. That center tier can even have different pacing from those surrounding it. In fact, that's why I use it. For the artist, this approach allows you to direct the readers eye exactly the way you want without anything extraneous.

The overall effect is like a Sergio Leone film – the sudden, jumbled violence, all the reaction shots, the isolated details.

Exactly. The last panel is an example of something I've done a lot in THE PATH, where I'm changing panel sizes to focus on small extraneous actions that aren't necessarily part of the main scene, but could be occurring simultaneously elsewhere. In this case, these guys have sat and done nothing, but they're in the same room. Yet, by changing the panel size, you're pulling out of the one action and refocusing on something else.

The aim of this spread is to show the chaos and quickness of battle without being graphic. You don't really ever see anything. You see guys moving. You see flashes of black. You see a sword. You see feet. But you never see a sword going through a man's body and his guts gushing out onto the floor.

In the spread above, the large panel that establishes the setting of the whole scene is depicted in the middle of the page – Obo-san preparing Todosi's body for burial. You see that there are guards around. Wulf and Aiko are waiting patiently. They're having a conversation about Obo-san and what's going on. At the same time Obo-san is preparing his brother's body. So in smaller inset panels I showed the calm, quiet preparations. In the larger panels, where the conversation's going on, you have a different pace. I kept all the conversation panels the same size, and the same placement of the two panel types has a calming feeling. There are no panel size changes. It's all kind of harmonious.

Is there a significance to the symmetry of the page? Do you vary according to mood?

Right, because I'm going for a different mood. The symmetry of this spread and the flat nature of the layout has an underlying calming effect. There's nothing jarring about any of the placements of the figures. There's nothing the reader has to work at. It's all pretty simple and straightforward.

Compare that to the other spread. There's a lot of changes in panel size. It's asymmetrical. Everything's tight within the panels, which leads you to feel there's more going on and you're missing stuff. Until the penultimate panel with Todosi, which is simple and bold and utterly calm.

The job of the graphic storyteller is to control not just the pacing but the time, the actual amount of time covered by the story. That's in the page layout as opposed to the panels. So designing the page is the first step in controlling time, the mood, and the overall energy level.

It seems like there's a lot of contraction and expansion of time throughout the book.

Yes. Very consciously. At least that's my goal. It all serves the story.

Symmetrical doesn't always mean sedate. Here's a page that is relatively symmetrical, but with an extremely violent action. One of the reasons I chose a symmetrical layout for the suicide scene is that I wanted to portray the naturalness of this act for these people. It wasn't an unnatural act, but part of their society. It was violent, but there's a calmness.

I focus on the swords in the first couple of panels rather than faces. Even though they're preparing for this bloody act, the establishing shot in the upper right gets across its ritual nature.

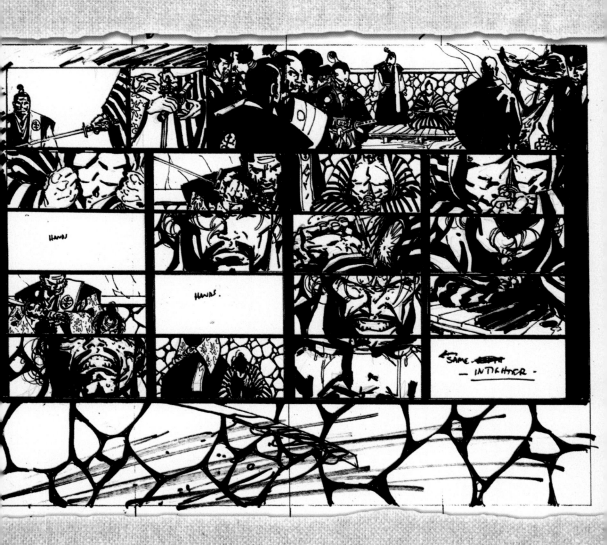

NEXT TIME

NEGATION
Chapter 10

It's the Match of the Century:
Baby Memi vs. Charon! While
Kaine & Co. search desperately,
the youngest abductee must
face the Lord of Negation
Space... alone!

Negation: Lawbringer

In this tale of Negation past,
we meet a young Charon and
his long-forgotten second
in command.

CRUX
Chapter 17

The newly-awakened Atlantean Aristophanes finds himself
alone in the Negation universe — and he's just irritated enough
to blow away some Negation troops.

SOJOURN
Chapters 13 & 14

A very special episode of Sojourn gives us a rare glimpse
into the family life of Bohr the troll. Then Arwyn and Gareth
take their quest to the catacombs of Ankhara.

IN FORGE 8

MERIDIAN
Chapter 28

Just as she's starting to feel down, Sephie discovers her father's old logbook, which holds valuable lessons for facing her new challenges as Minister of Meridian.

ROUTE 666
Chapter 2

Escaping the asylum was easy for Cassie, at least compared to life on the run with no money, no friends, and no one who believes there are spirits out to steal her soul.

THE PATH
Chapter 7

It's war as Shinacea invades, with only the remnants of Nayado's samurai to stop it. Will Obo-san step between the warring armies?

EDGE 7

EDGE

MONTHLY COMICS FOR YOUR BOOKSHELF™

RUSE
Chapter 10

SIGIL
Chapter 26

SCION
Chapter 27

MYSTIC
Chapter 25

Way of the Rat
Chapters 3 & 4

The First
Chapter 20

ON SALE OCTOBER 30TH

CROSSGEN COMICS

Graphic Novels

THE FIRST 1	Two Houses Divided	$19.95	1-931484-04-X
THE FIRST 2	Magnificent Tension	$19.95	1-931484-17-1
MYSTIC 1	Rite of Passage	$19.95	1-931484-00-7
MYSTIC 2	The Demon Queen	$19.95	1-931484-06-6
MYSTIC 3	Siege of Scales	$15.95	1-931484-24-4
MERIDIAN 1	Flying Solo	$19.95	1-931484-03-1
MERIDIAN 2	Going to Ground	$19.95	1-931484-09-0
MERIDIAN 3	Taking the Skies	$15.95	1-931484-21-X
SCION 1	Conflict of Conscience	$19.95	1-931484-02-3
SCION 2	Blood for Blood	$19.95	1-931484-08-2
SCION 3	Divided Loyalties	$15.95	1-931484-26-0
SIGIL 1	Mark of Power	$19.95	1-931484-01-5
SIGIL 2	The Marked Man	$19.95	1-931484-07-4
SIGIL 3	The Lizard God	$15.95	1-931484-28-7
CRUX 1	Atlantis Rising	$15.95	1-931484-14-7
NEGATION 1	Bohica!	$19.95	1-931484-30-9
SOJOURN 1	From the Ashes	$19.95	1-931484-15-5
SOJOURN 2	The Dragon's Tale	$15.95	1-931484-34-1
RUSE 1	Enter the Detective	$15.95	1-931484-19-8
THE PATH 1	Crisis of Faith	$19.95	1-931484-32-5
CROSSGEN ILLUSTRATED Volume 1		$24.95	1-931484-05-8

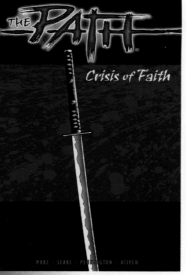

Crisis of Faith
THE PATH Volume 1
192 Pages • $19.95
ISBN 1-931484-32-5

The first collection of CrossGen's smash hit samurai series mixes swordplay and magic in an explosive combination. Written by Ron Marz with art by Bart Sears

The Dragon's Tale
SOJOURN Volume 2
160 Pages • $15.95
ISBN 1-931484-34-1

The archer Arwyn finds an unlikely ally in her quest to slay the dread Mordath. Will she win this battle? Written by Ron Marz with art by Wizard Top 10 Artist Greg Land

BOHICA!
NEGATION Volume 1
192 Pages • $19.95
ISBN 1-931484-30-9

Kidnapped and stranded in a universe of evil, Obregon Kaine knows the only way home is to topple a God! Written by Tony Bedard with art by Paul Pelletier